A Deal With The Devil

A. Carys

A. Carys

The characters and events portrayed in this book are fictitious. Any similarity to real persons, living or dead, is coincidental and not intended by the author.

No part of this book may be reproduced, or stored in a retrieval system, or transmitted in any form or by any means, electronic, mechanical, photocopying, recording, or otherwise, without express written permission of the publisher.

Copyright © 2024 A. Carys

All rights reserved.

BOOKS IN THIS SERIES

Of Doors and Betrayal

The Pickpocket and the Princess

The Master, My Wings, Our Service

'Cos This Is How Villains Are Made

A Circus of Wonder

A Sentence to Death

A Deal With The Devil

Let Her Go

The Three

Queen Rory, The Banished

A. Carys

DEDICATION

I'm waiting for something exciting…

A. Carys

CHAPTER ONE

I feel numb as I sit and stare at the ceiling of my bedroom.

It's been twelve hours since he died, and ten hours since I shut myself in my room. I've left this bed twice in those ten hours. The first time was to grab a small bowl of rice and steamed vegetables that had been left outside my door, the second was to use the bathroom.

The events of the day keep playing on my mind. Over and over on a loop. It's left me with a splitting headache and no amount of painkillers seem to be able to shift it. I want the pain in my head to stop, to leave me alone so that I can grieve in peace. It feels like it's torturing me because I wasn't quick enough. I was nearly quick enough though, but nearly quick enough never saved anybody.

"I was right there," I mutter again.

I was in the dungeon ready to get Jake, and as many others, out of there. But when I got to the cells, they were gone. I could've intercepted them as they were walking through the House but I couldn't because Dorian locked me in one of the cells, and in that moment, I've never wanted to kill anyone more.

I reach the bottom of the hallway and run straight past the first three cells, heading straight for the fourth cell.

"Jake!" I call out, my shouts echoing off the stone walls. "Jake!" I call again.

There's no response.

I step closer to the cell before pushing at the bars. They swing open slowly, revealing what I dreaded the most; an empty cell. I step inside and carefully look at the two beds. The light is dim so it's hard to see much, but something crunches under my boot. I bend down and feel around for the item. My fingers brush over the item and I pick it up.

I have to bring it up close to my eyes to be able to

make out any details, but when my eyes focus, I realise that it's a bracelet, but not just any bracelet. I have the same one, a piece of thin, braided rope with a bead on either end. A silly bracelet my classmates and I made when we were at the Academy. Rydell, me, Alex, Sean, Thea and Jake. Our small group of friends, siblings even, if I was going to get soppy. Together we challenged each other, raised each other up and supported one other.

A shuffling behind me catches my attention. I turn, being careful not to make too much noise. I tiptoe over to the far wall and lean against it in the hope of concealing myself in the shadows.

Another noise fills the silence, this time from the right. I try to scan the area in front of me but the darkness is too much. All I can see are fuzzy circles from where my eyes haven't adjusted.

"Etta?" I query, just in case she's come to find me. Which, when I think about it, is highly unlikely because she should be in the arena keeping an eye on everything.

Something moves in the corridor outside of the cell, I catch it just out of the corner of my eye. My heartbeat feels like it's in my throat and my mouth suddenly becomes dry. I need to get going. Jake isn't down here and I'm wasting time.

I step toward the cell door but it slams shut in my face, and I hear the unmistakable clunk of a lock. I grip the bars and shake the door.

"Whoever you are, this isn't funny," I say as I briefly catch a glance of something moving in front of me.

"I didn't take you as one to be spooked by the dark, Ilana," a voice says from the shadows. A voice that I recognise, and the person it belongs to will be in serious trouble once this is over.

"Dorian, let me out."

"I need to talk to you."

I scoff. "I'm a little preoccupied right now."

"I know, but we never got to finish our conversation at the Archives."

"I'm in the middle of something," I repeat in the hopes of highlighting the urgency of the situation.

"There are lives at stake here, Ilana."

"I know that."

"Unfortunately, there's nothing you can do about

it. Believe me, I've already tried."

"What do you mean you've already tried? What have you been keeping from us Dorian?"

"It's not a punishment in the way that you're thinking. I'm sorry, Ilana, but the prisoners won't be coming back to these cells."

My words get caught in my throat.

"You're lying," I manage to choke out.

"I wish I was, but the Father changed his mind after the parade. He says it's a life for a life. The Defectors' new and current lives are being traded for the lives of their descendants."

"Dorian. I swear on the Bones, let me out of here."

"I will. But I need to tell you that Adeem will be back soon to cash in the other job that–"

I roll my eyes and cut him off. "I'm aware of that, Dorian. Now let me out."

"I didn't finish. When he does, let me know, because I have a feeling we'll be after similar things."

"I don't care what Adeem is going to ask of me, just let me out."

"I will. Just tell me you'll let me know what he asks of you."

I grit my teeth, but I know this is a losing battle. "Fine. I'll tell you. Now let me out of this bloody cell."

He unlocks the door and I step out; I go to move further down the corridor but he grabs my wrist.

"I hope you know that I tried to stop this from getting worse," he says.

I don't say anything in return as I yank my wrist from his grip and sprint away.

"Ilana?" Beck calls from the other side of my bedroom door.

"Come in," I say, not looking away from the ceiling.

I see the door open out of my peripheral vision and Beck steps into the room. He doesn't say anything as he shuts the door behind him. I look back to the ceiling and the only indication that he's moved closer to the bed is when it dips next to me.

"We're going to hold a vigil for Jake. Would you like to join?"

I nod but I don't look at him. I feel him softly grab my wrist before he gently tries to pull me from the bed. I shift but let him drag me to the edge of the bed. I take a deep breath, sit up and swing my legs over the side of the bed before grabbing Jake's bracelet from my nightstand.

"Come on," he gently mutters as he loops his arm through mine. He guides me off the bed and out of my room. He helps me down the stairs and out into the main area of the club before telling me to sit on one of the chairs opposite the fireplace.

For a moment, I sit with my eyes locked on the bracelet in my hand. Doubt floods through me and the thoughts that rush through my head are anything but gentle. I don't think I can do this, sit here and take part in the vigil. I don't think I can sit here and think about Jake without breaking down. Everything feels too raw, too fresh, but the second my eyes catch sight of the golden mantel that encases the fireplace, I know that this is something I must do.

My eyes travel along the mantel, and they land on a sketch of Jake in a wooden frame. I recognise the image; it was attached to the manila folder I was given upon arriving back in Corvian. He's wearing a neutral expression, but the shine in his eye that the artist managed to capture tells me that this was sketched on our first day in camp. I remember standing behind the artist, pulling faces at him, trying to distract him. He wouldn't crack though, wouldn't let his facial expression change, but the glint of being entertained sat in his eyes, and the artist managed to capture it.

My eyes leave the frame and travel to the shelf that has been hung from the mantle. The shelf holds items ready for a Mourning Ritual. This isn't going to just be a vigil; it's going to be a time to let go. To bring forth the feelings of pain and sorrow and rid ourselves of them. I see why Beck told me it was a vigil; I never would've left my room if I'd known he wanted to perform a Mourning Ritual. I would've told him to leave me be. To let me stew in my feelings for a little bit longer.

A hand running over the back of my head draws my attention from the shelf.

"Stop overthinking, just relax," Beck says as he walks over to the shelf.

"You could've told me it was a ritual."

"And have you tell me to shove it where the sun

doesn't shine?"

I shake my head, a faint smile pulling at my lips.

It's not long until Etta, Ty and Laurie sit down on the chairs next to me. Beck follows suit after he's sorted out the items on the shelf, items that are required for a Mourning Ritual.

Four stems of lavender.

Three candles.

An array of human bones.

In Bordovan culture, bones are used in worship, prayer, death and fortune telling. Bordovan gods are sometimes referred to as the Bones. The moniker plays into the sacredness of bones in our religious beliefs, and tonight we'll say prayers over them.

We join hands for a moment, to signal the beginning of the Ritual. I assume that Beck has cleared the club of its staff and patrons. For this Ritual, you and the others who wish to take part must be alone. To be without interference from other energies that may interfere with the process.

We start with a joint prayer. A prayer which we all know, one that is famously taught during Religious Studies in schools. It's an address to the spirits who will guide the Ritual, who will answer to the energy that we put out there.

The Ritual is made up of three steps; the praying slash asking, which we've already done, the lighting and the burning. Since we've done the praying, we move onto the lighting of the candles. Ty stands and takes a match. He strikes it and touches it to the candle wicks. Once all three are lit, we begin saying a phrase that wishes for the person who is being prayed for to 'pass over to the other side safely'.

En orr soulle tasp asfley ofro ell oland se ell givan op ell oland se ell decess.
En ær ista passuno, hra yna vilgilan enkat ni orr amne astifi ell estlensess ni orr soulle.

I get up from my chair and move toward the candles. I take hold of the bracelet that I found in the cell and offer it to the candles. When it comes to death, offering the Bones something of the deceased is meant to show peace. To show that the loss of that person can be accepted and respected.

Leaving the bracelet to be eaten by the flames, I

return to my seat. Etta takes hold of my hand, squeezing it tightly as we wait for the bracelet to become nothing but embers.

It takes a while, but once the bracelet has disintegrated, we all raise a glass to Jake. Remembering who he was as a person and celebrating his life. We leave the candles burning as we move quietly around each other as we work to open the club for the evening rush. It's important that after the ritual, you step back into your daily routine, or as close to a familiar routine as possible. I work on setting up each table, tucking the chairs underneath the tables before setting them with pitchers of water and ashtrays.

I then help with serving the customers, and I notice I feel lighter. The ritual has allowed the grief I am feeling to lessen and to be redirected to those who will guide Jake through the next part of his life.

CHAPTER TWO

Life, after the death of a friend or loved one, does carry on. Keeping busy in the club is something that has kept my mind from drifting to the visions of Jake's final moments. The moments where the blindfold was pulled over his eyes and the guards cocked their guns. The way everyone in the crowd clapped and cheered—I shake my head and try to steer my thoughts back to the task in front of me.

Getting back into a normal routine has been my main goal, so every morning, I get up at the first light of dawn, change my clothes and head down to the bar to start preparing for the day. It's become a routine, a steady and controlled way of overcoming the sadness and grief that catches up to me at night-time.

"If you keep cleaning that one spot, you're gonna

wear away the varnish," Ty says as he takes a seat at one of the bar stools, placing his plate of toast down in front of him.

"And if I do, I'll be sure to lather the wood with your disgusting hair gel," I respond as I steal a piece of toast, biting off one of the corners.

He huffs and sticks his tongue out at me. "That's rude, and that's my piece of toast."

"Not anymore," I mumble as I eat the bread while tucking the wet cloth and cleaning supplies back under the bar.

We bicker back and forth for a few minutes until Beck emerges from the stairs and strolls to stand beside Ty. He scolds us both for arguing over a piece of toast before sending Ty shopping with Leo.

Leo works for Beck, he's the Bar and Floor Manager for the Skull and Bone. He worked in the bar long before we all managed to scrounge up enough money to buy the original owners out. He was a loyal employee then and is still a loyal employee now, almost five years later. When we took over, we made it clear that we weren't going to be changing the staff that worked here. We only hired new staff after some of the original staff members decided they didn't want to work for Beck. They didn't want to work for a man who was, essentially, a criminal, but Leo has remained with us and has become an honorary Bonesman. We trust him implicitly with our bar and our secrets, and his loyalty has proved to be unmatched. No matter the number of bars, restaurants, hotels or hostels that try to poach him, he always decides to stay. But Leo isn't as young as he was and that means Beck always sends someone with him to take on the heavy lifting of the groceries.

"Why me? Send Lana, she took *my* toast."

Beck sighs and rolls his eyes. "Ty, I really don't give a shit that she took your toast. We share with each other all the time, so get over it, and go help Leo with the shopping. A carriage will be here for you in fifteen minutes."

Ty makes a huffing sound before sliding off his stool and heading toward the back of the club, taking his plate with him.

"For the love of Bones, do you have to take his breakfast?"

I shrug. "It was one corner of one piece of toast.

He brought out three pieces."

Beck sighs and runs his hands down his face. "You're both twenty-six yet you still act like children."

I shrug and jump up backwards from where I'm leaning against the bar. I plant myself on the wooden countertop and spin round, my boots coming to rest on the bar stool next to Beck.

"Sorry," I mutter, even though I know Beck isn't mad at me. "Have there been any more updates?"

Beck shakes his head. "The House seems to have finished punishing the descendants. But saying that, I have Lola, Kyle and Mikhale watching the ports throughout the day before James, Ella and Ben take over tonight. Etta is coordinating with them after their shift changes and collecting any notes they took. Everything is under control. If the House tries to do that again, we'll know."

I nod. "Thank you."

The door to the club bangs open. We turn.

"Dorian, I don't care what you have or don't have going on in your life, but it doesn't mean that you need to come and spy on my *private* meetings."

"*Ih lepsay*. It wasn't a private meeting. You were having it out in the open, swapping notes and secrets. That's not private, that's sloppy."

I watch Etta shake with rage. She hates Dorian, possibly even more than I do, but Beck insisted that he become a half member of the Skulls. Apparently, he's useful, but I'm yet to see him prove that claim. But at the end of the day, I trust Beck's decisions and that's all that matters.

"Do you know what happened to the last person that insulted me? Called me out in public and got in the middle of something that doesn't concern them?" she asks as she sizes up to Dorian.

"No. Why don't you show me?" he challenges, which is his most stupid move to date because I catch a glimpse of Bolt, Etta's cat, moving along the edge of the shadows.

"Beck," I mutter.

"Already on it," he mutters back as he swiftly moves behind the bar and out to the other side so that he is standing behind Etta.

"Anyone ever tell you not to pick fights with those who have more power than you?"

Dorian laughs. "No. I fight whoever I want. So come on then, *Enfreynar*, fight me."

Hellhound. It was her nickname for her entire childhood and to call her it is like signing your own death certificate. While she is a loyal friend and an excellent partner in crime, she holds quite the vicious streak. She used that streak her entire childhood, it was her crutch, her only support system she had against her family. A family who never hesitated to remind her that she was a product of her father's transgressions in her parent's marriage. And what didn't help was the development of her mutant ability. She's able to move with the speed of a cheetah and the grace of a ballerina. She's violence and stealth wrapped into one and a dangerous opponent to take on.

Etta launches herself at Dorian, quickly taking the advantage as she feigns jumping upwards before she slides down and between his legs. She twists herself onto her knees before jabbing the sides of her hands into his knees. He crumples to the floor and Etta prepares for her next attack when Beck grabs her around the waist, holding her against him as he tells her to calm down.

"Aw, come on Beck. Don't stop the fight now, we were just getting started," Dorian teases as he steps forward, bringing his face level with Etta's. I never heard a human snarl before, but I'm pretty sure it's what Etta does as she gnashes her teeth at him.

"Scary," he teases and in the next moment, time moves far too quickly as Bolts jumps and swings his claws at Dorian. He manages to catch Dorian's cheek, leaving three long and jagged cuts on his face. He stumbles backwards and Bolt hops up on the bar counter before sauntering over to me.

"You're a good boy," I coo as I reach into the little pot of cat treats we keep behind the bar.

"Who lets animals roam in a business where food is served?" Dorian says, seething as he gently touches his cheek.

"We do because Bolt is part of the family," Etta says as she still fights against Beck's hold.

"It's unsanitary," Dorian mutters as he disappears to the back, probably in search of a tissue or two.

I turn my attention to Beck and Etta.

"If I let you go, will you behave? That means no

more attacking Dorian until you are *outside* of my club," Beck scolds.

"I'll behave," she mutters.

"Sorry, I couldn't hear you."

"I'll behave," she says, a lot louder this time and Beck nods.

"Good child," he smirks and only just manages to duck out of the way as Etta turns and throws a punch.

"I swear on the Bon–" She's cut off as Beck grabs her arms, pulls them behind her back and restrains her against the bar.

"What did I just say?" Beck grits.

"You called me a child."

"Because you're behaving like one."

"Are you two finished?" Dorian asks as he emerges from the back, the cuts on his face no longer bleeding.

Beck lets go of Etta, but not before whispering something in her ear which makes them both smirk. Beck, as demonstrated, is the leader of the Skulls. He's a good boss and he rules with fairness and justice, unlike a lot of the gangs around Bordova. But being fair and just doesn't mean he is weak. He will happily put a traitor in the ground without a second thought.

But everything he just did with Etta is similar to that of a sibling battle. Laurie, Etta, myself, Ty, Beck and Maven all grew up together. We view each other like siblings, with Beck as the oldest and most responsible. The rest of us happily squabble like little children and Beck sorts it out. Unfortunately, Maven made an enemy of the wrong person and was killed just over twelve years ago. It was a sad day, an awful day, but we rose from the ashes. We officially formed the Skulls, the name was an idea given to us by Maven before he passed, and we became a gang that was ready to take over the country. The rumours that surround us are what have kept us so feared in the community. We keep a skull in plain view of the customers and the rumour that it is the skull of the man who killed Maven is what keeps most people from crossing us. It's not actually the man's skull, just a random one we found, but no one wants to have their bones on display for all to see, and that's enough motivation to keep them in their lanes.

"Yeah, we're finished," Beck says as he comes

back behind the bar. He pushes me slightly to the side so that he can stand directly behind Bolt and begins stroking him. I glare at Dorian as he takes a seat in front of me.

"Good. I have some information that you will be interested in."

I raise an eyebrow. "Oh yeah? And what is this information?"

"Adeem Anson is back in town."

CHAPTER THREE

I wouldn't ever think that Dorian is right, and I definitely wouldn't say it to his face. But for once, he is, and by the late afternoon, we are graced with Adeem's presence as he steps through the doors to the club.

"Bordova, ever the country of warm welcomes," he says as he takes a seat in the biggest booth we have.

I roll my eyes before heading over to him, but not before tapping Beck on the shoulder and gesturing for him to come with me. He excuses himself from the conversation he's having and follows me over. We take a seat opposite Adeem and wait for him to begin.

"Miss Kiri, you're looking ever so vibrant today. May I ask the secret?"

I raise an eyebrow at him. "Sleep. Prayer. Fighting with people much bigger than me."

He chuckles. "Of course. And Beck, your businesses are thriving, what's the secret there?"

"Respect, keeping my business to myself. No one asking me about my secrets."

"Ever the friendly businessman. Anyway, I assume you know why I'm here."

I nod. "I guess it has something to do with the backstabbing you did during your last visit."

"Backstabbing? No. Business? Yes."

"I got you that bloody necklace. I was lucky I managed to convince Alik that those weren't my blades."

"There is no luck in this business, Miss Kiri. Only survival."

I roll my eyes and I feel Beck place his hand on my knee. A subtle order to remain calm, that or an attempt to hold me back from launching myself across the table. "You didn't come here to give me guidance on my lifestyle, so please, move on to why you are here," I grit out as politely as possible.

Adeem smiles. "I'm interested in cashing your

second payment."

"Okay," I say, nodding.

"What's the job?" Beck asks.

He shakes his head. "So eager. But I won't tell you until later tonight during dinner here at the Skull and Bone. I will only share the details if every single member of your crew is here. That includes the Rau siblings."

I grit my teeth. "Half eleven, just after closing," I offer and I see Beck subtly nod out of the corner of my eye.

"Perfect. See you then." And with that, Adeem saunters out of the club and into the busy streets of Bordova.

"I really hate that man," Beck says as he gets out of the booth.

"You and me both."

CHAPTER FOUR

The day passes relatively slowly.

Waiting for the clock to strike half eleven is torture. The desperation to know what Adeem wants from us has been gnawing away at me for the better part of the day.

"What's this?" I ask as Beck hands me a piece of paper, his handwriting scrawled all over it.

"A to-do list."

"Why can't Ty do this?"

"Your restlessness is making the place look untidy. This list should keep you preoccupied until the meeting."

"I'm not a child. I'm more than capable of keeping myself entertained."

He raises an eyebrow. "Take the list, do the jobs."

"Is that an order?"

He shoots me a glare, one that I know means Leader Beck has taken over. I nod and walk out from behind the bar. I stop in front of him and make a show of plucking the list from his hand.

"Thank you."

"Do you use your boss's voice with Lila?" I ask cheekily before turning on my heel.

"I use my boss' voice when my employees try to defy my orders."

I smile. "Isn't Lila an employee?"

He runs a hand down his face and sighs. "Just go and complete the list."

I laugh as I walk out of the club and into the busy streets of Bordova.

By the time I return, it's already seven–o–clock and the evening rush is already in full swing. I quickly dive behind the bar and take over a portion of the customers from Ty. The night seems to drag as we serve wave after wave of customers. But as the night slowly draws to a close, the customers start to filter out and we have the chance to breathe.

"Thanks for the help," Ty says as he tidies away a stack of freshly cleaned glasses.

"No problem," I respond.

We continue to swap between cleaning glasses and serving the customers their final drinks until eleven fifteen, which is when Beck and Etta start letting the customers know it's time to think about leaving. Two Bonesmen, our security who stand in front of the doors, help usher out the stragglers who try to stay past closing.

"You know, we'll miss having you help out when you go back to Corvian," Ty says as he wipes down the countertop.

I pull my lips into a fine line, not having planned on telling them my plans yet.

"What?" he quickly says at the sight of my facial expression.

I sigh and put down the tray of glasses in my hand. "I'm not going back to Corvian, at least not in the professional sense."

Everyone stops what they are doing.

"What do you mean?" Laurie asks.

"I do need to go back at some point to iron out all

of the details, but I don't think I'll be going back to my role in the army."

"Really?" Etta asks, coming closer to me.

"Yeah. I don't want to go back. It's silly, but the people I work with know that I tried to save Jake and the others, but I failed and I don't think I can face them. I want to live here with you guys, for as long as you'll have me."

Etta jumps and wraps her arms around my neck, nearly toppling me over. It's been a while since I stayed in Bordova for a prolonged period of time. Despite all the holidays that James and Phillip brought us on, I never got to stay with my friends. With my second family.

"We'd be over the moon to have you back with us Lana," Beck says as he joins in the hug. This wasn't at all how I had planned on sharing this news, but everyone seems happy as they pile on top of Etta and I.

Everyone is laughing and murmuring about what we can all do once I'm back here for good. We're so lost in our own happiness that we don't hear the opening of the front door.

"Oh, this looks lovely. What are we celebrating?" Adeem asks, bursting our bubble of joy.

"Nothing that concerns you," I say as everyone peels away.

"So abrasive, Kiri. There's no need for it."

I raise an eyebrow at him and he shakes head before heading back to the same booth he sat in earlier today.

"Well, shall we get started? Time is a sensitive matter in this case."

I shrug and head over to the booth. I'm closely followed by Etta and Beck while Laurie and Ty grab the food platters Leo kindly assembled for us.

"Where are the other two? The Rau siblings?"

"They'll be here."

Adeem nods.

As we wait for Dorian and Grace, we tuck into the food. Three different cheeses, all cut into thin slices or tiny cubes. Olives with wooden skewers and a selection of meats that have been cut into circles for easy consumption. There's also sticks of lightly toasted bread that have been slathered with melted garlic butter and other herbs, alongside a selection of raw vegetables and a chickpea sauce for them to be dipped into.

As we're eating, Grace and Dorian walk in. Everyone shuffles up in the booth so that they can sit down. Beck hands them both plates so that they can start eating.

"Now that you're all here I can give you the details of the job," Adeem says, breaking the silence.

"Okay, tell us then," Etta says, clearly getting impatient with all of the unnecessary pauses Adeem adds into his sentences.

"I need you to steal two paintings from the House on the night of the Diplomatic Mutuals Meeting. It's in one week and it's the only night in which the building will be vulnerable."

"What's the Diplomatic Mutuals Meeting?" Ty asks.

"It's a night where Diplomats from countries across the world come and spend the evening together. They talk about all kinds of important things like trade deals, alliances and ways to better the way they live rather than focusing on the lives of the people they are in charge of," Grace explains.

"So, you want us to take two paintings while this event is going on?" Beck asks.

Adeem nods. "Yes. I have two forgeries for you to replace them with."

"What's the significance of the paintings?" Etta asks, eyeing Adeem.

"They previously belonged to the Altaineian Royal family. They were taken during the Bordovan siege a little over nineteen years ago. I have been tasked with retrieving them since I have a particular talent for securing rare and untouchable items."

"And that's where we come in?" I ask.

"Exactly. And since Dorian and Grace are children of the Father, they will be key to getting you in."

"Royals, eh?" Beck teases and raises an eyebrow.

"There's no need to argue right now, please do that once I have left."

I roll my eyes.

"I take it you've already come up with a plan?" I question as I push my plate away from me.

Adeem nods and takes us through his preliminary plan, leaving us with it written down in bullet points along with maps and blueprints of the House. He hands out specific tasks and takes us through the exchange process post-job. Once the meeting draws to a close, we escort Adeem to the carriage that is waiting for him before heading back into the club.

CHAPTER FIVE

Three days.

That's how long we've been trying to come up with a plausible plan to get into the House. We've thrown around countless hypothetical ideas but none of them worked when we played them out. We used the guard rotas and security placements to act out breaking in, and so far, the person breaking in has been caught every single time.

"What if we go in through the ceiling windows and then we use the support beams to navigate our way through the House? Quick and easy," Ty offers as he rocks backwards on his chair.

"Are you stupid?" Etta scoffs.

"No," he answers with a silly tone before falling backwards off his chair as the back legs give out from underneath him. He falls with a thud and Etta bursts out laughing. I shake my head with a smile.

"What have I told you about rocking on your chair?" Laurie asks as he helps Ty up.

"Don't know and it's not the time for a lecture."

"But–" Laurie starts but he gets cut off by Dorian.

"I could take one person as my guest. Introduce them as my partner and we'd probably be able to get away with roaming the palace. Everyone else would have to find their own way in."

"What if I took a couple of friends? Da isn't going to question it, he knows I love to have my friends at these events so he wouldn't bat an eyelid," suggests Grace.

Dorian nods. "That's true. How many do you think you could take?"

"Probably two, anymore and that'll definitely raise some eyebrows," she says.

Dorian nods. "Well, if you took Ty and Etta then I could take Ilana. Beck and Laurie, you'd have to find your own way in."

I raise my eyebrows at him. "No. No way. I'll take my chances."

Beck comes back over to the table we're sitting at. "Lana, I know you and Dorian aren't on the greatest of terms right now, but this is our best chance at getting into the House. We want Adeem gone as soon as possible, so please, let Dorian take you as his guest."

I shoot him a pointed look before sighing. "Fine. But I want it known that I hate him and if he crosses me, I'm going to kill him."

"Noted," he says with a nod.

"We're going to have a lot of fun," Dorian says and I playfully but not-so-playfully punch him on the arm.

"Anyway," Beck says, drawing our attention away from trying to maim each other. "That leaves me and Laurie with no way in."

"Ac-actually I can get us in," Laurie stutters.

"How?" Dorian asks and I roll my eyes at his blatant stupid question.

"Owin O-Shin is my father. He's the political liaison between Bordova and Madoneia."

"So that's getting inside of the event sorted, but there's still other factors we haven't considered. What will we wear? How will we get the paintings without being seen, and to piggy back off that question, how will we get out without being seen?" Beck asks as he goes over to the table where the blue prints and maps have been laid out.

"Leave all of that with Ilana and I. We'll get the paintings and get them out as well. You guys will just need to create a distraction."

"Oh yeah? And what will that distraction be?" I ask, turning to look at Dorian.

Dorian smiles. "A very good, crowd gathering distraction."

CHAPTER SIX

Four days later...

In four hours, I will be inside of the House.

We're leaving Leo in charge of the club while we're out. Lauren, Amelia and Benji, who are our supervisors, will be helping. They're all under strict instructions to only serve patrons and members tonight. Tourists and infrequent flyers are to be turned away at the door. The last thing we need is randoms coming in and picking fights with each other while we're away.

"How long does it take for them to pick up an order?" Ty asks as we sit in a booth.

Etta, Ty, Laurie, Beck and myself are all sitting in a booth toward the front of the club. We're having a small and slightly alcoholic drink to help soothe our nerves. We're also waiting for Grace and Dorian to arrive with our outfits. They left early this morning and have yet to return.

While we've been waiting, Amelia pinned Etta's hair into an updo while Lauren worked on mine, twisting and curling it onto plastic tubes. My hair is still attached to these tubes and won't be taken out until just before we leave. I hate them, it feels like I'm balancing bricks on the top of my head, but Lauren insisted that it was the only other way to curl my hair that didn't involve plaits.

"They'll be here soon," I say before finishing my drink in a single gulp.

Nervous is the wrong word for what I'm feeling, but I'm struggling to think of a better word to describe the feelings that are brewing inside of me. I've done jobs like this before. We used to break in and steal things all the time when we were younger. It was our way of helping our families with money, and the Bones know that I tried to help my parents with their debts. But this is a high-risk job. If we get caught in the act, we'll be shot on sight. And if we're not shot on sight, we'll be arrested before serving the death penalty. So, the punishment of doing this wrong severely outweighs the perks of being free from Adeem.

"We're here, we're here," Grace yells as she stumbles through the doors. We all stand and go over to her as Dorian enters.

"What took you so long?" Beck asks as he takes one of the bagged hangers from her.

"Many things. Da wanted us to help set up and then he had us running around the palace trying to find members of staff. It's a mess over there, but we managed to slip away," Dorian says as both of them place down garment bags.

"The outfits are in those bags," says Grace.

We nod and head to the bags. I'm the first one there and I quickly riffle through them until I find my one. I grab it by the coat hanger and head straight for the stairs. My room is the second one from the top step so I quickly duck into it. I push the door too before I unzip the bag and carefully pull out the most breath-taking dress, I think I've ever laid my eyes on.

"Bloody hell," I mutter as I hook the hanger over my curtain rail.

Taking a step back, I admire the outfit. Deep,

royal blue fabric forms the base of a very detailed corset. Grey flowers and delicate lace decorate the cups and bodice of the corset. The patterns swirl down onto the trousers. The trousers are made of silk under material that has been covered in tulle to make them look like a flowy skirt. The outfit is stunning, and as I take it down off the coat hanger, the cape that's been draped over the corset's zip catches my eye. It's the same deep blue as the corset and it comes together at the top of what I assume to be a choker that will sit around my neck.

I slip out of the loose trousers and jumper I'm wearing. I fold them up and place them at the edge of my bed before undoing the zip and stepping into the body suit. I pull it all the way up before taking off my bra and securing the corset over my chest. I reach around and try to do up the zip. I move the zip a little bit but I can't get it up further than my waist.

"Etta?" I call out.

"Etta, can you come and help me please?" I shout and the door to my room opens not even a second later.

"You called for help?" a voice says. A deep voice

which doesn't belong to Etta. I whip round and see Dorian standing there dressed in a suit the same colour as my outfit.

"Not from you."

"Everyone else is busy."

I grit my teeth. "Fine. Could you zip us the back of my corset? I can't reach it."

"Say please."

I raise an eyebrow at him. "Please?" I say mockingly.

He smiles and comes over. I turn my back to him and shiver when I feel one of his hands gently gather each side of the corset. I feel him pull them toward each other before pulling the zip up. The corset tightens and I step away the second he stops pulling at the zip.

"Thanks," I mutter.

I reach for the cape but Dorian seems to have the same idea as he reaches for it as well. He beats me to it and moves it out of my grasp as I try to snatch it from him. He opens the choker at the top and motions for me to turn. I almost protest, but I've no clue how the clasp works so I'd have to call for more help. I turn and watch his hands appear either side of my neck.

"Hold," he orders and I grab the ends of the choker. He comes to stand in front of me and tightens the choker so that it won't slip. I feel my heart rate pick up as a sliver of panic starts to rise inside of me. The closeness of Dorian's hands to my neck has set me on edge because if he wanted to strangle me, he wouldn't have to try very hard.

"I'm not going to strangle you."

"Not what I was thinking about."

"Liar."

"Fuck you."

He laughs. "You're so easy to rile up. You should work on that Lana."

"It's Ilana to you."

He shrugs and moves over to the bed. "I forgot to give you these earlier. I saw them and I thought they'd go with your outfit."

He hands me a shoe box which I hadn't seen him bring in with him. I open the box and pull out a pair of boots. I look at him and nod in thanks before bending down to put them on. When I stand up, Dorian is no longer in the room and a small feeling of regret forms in my chest.

I could've been a little nicer, I think. But then again, he wasted my time when it came to trying to save Jake, and those minutes could've been the difference between saving him and not.

CHAPTER SEVEN

When it comes to travelling to the Diplomatic Mutuals Meetings, we separate into our groups. Myself and Dorian. Beck and Laurie. Etta, Ty and Grace.

On the way over, we discuss our cover story and come to the decision to say that we are dating. A secret relationship that the Father and the Mother have yet to hear about. Dorian told me that it would be easier to date, for lack of a better word, a commoner instead of another Royal. He seems far too enthusiastic about pretending to date me that I nearly refuse, but with a little persuasion, and some begging, he convinces me. We then go through our plan of attack, especially since Dorian and I have been given the responsibility of stealing the paintings. Apparently, Dorian is quite the chatterbox in the Royal social scenes, so him turning up at one of these events and not talking to people would be out of character. So, before we make a move to steal the paintings, we're going to mingle with the guests for a little while.

The door to the carriage opens and Dorian gets out first. He waits by the steps and offers me his hand. I take it and flash him a brief smile. From there, Dorian guides me inside of the House, his hand fixed on my lower back.

"Are you sure this will work?" I ask as we step into the ballroom.

"Of course. My parents haven't looked at the artwork in years, at least not in great detail. And they own so many that I'd be surprised if they noticed that two of them are forgeries."

I nod and take a deep breath. Dorian pulls me close as the crowd starts to form around us. I turn on my acting skills and stand there dutifully as he wraps an arm loosely around my waist. One of my hands goes around the back of him while the other rests gently on his waistcoat.

While he chats to the guests, I subtly observe the room. I start by watching the guard movements, making sure that the timings match the piece of paper Adeem had given us. There's two on each exit, with a patrolling distance of the two pillars either side of that exit. There's a total of eight exits, two on each wall of the ballroom. Sixteen guards with at least two reserves waiting down the corridor ready to intercept any stray guests who make it out of the ballroom.

I then move onto the Mother and the Father. It takes me a few seconds to find them, but when I do, they're both standing by their thrones. I watch them for a few seconds at a time, but they don't seem to venture very far into the room. The furthest they move from their thrones is to greet the guests who seem to be flocking to them in waves. Once the first wave of guests has cleared, the next lot flood towards them. It's like they're enchanted, like they're being pulled towards the Mother and the Father. It's strange to watch, but once I've got a good enough idea of what they're up to, I turn my attention to the guests. The ballroom is full of popular guests, clearly only invited to fill up the ballroom. There are well-known theatre actresses like Evalia Andreas, Ellie Whitaker and her rumoured, Madoneian crime-boss husband George Whitaker. There are also news page writers like Tia Salinger. Then there's the Diplomats, all who are easily identifiable. They're all dressed in fancy suits, their countries flags are emblazoned at the top of their arms. They also have their Diplomatic sashes and their service medals attached to the breast pockets of their blazers.

"Oh Dorian, I'm so happy you came," his mother says as she kisses his cheek.

"Couldn't miss my favourite event of the year," he responds half sarcastically.

"Dorian, behave," she playfully scolds, which makes his father smirk.

"He's like this all the time, always has a sarcastic response to everything I say," I tell his parents which draws their eyes from Dorian to me. I kindly smile at them and hold eye contact with his mother.

"Aren't you going to introduce us, son?" asks his father. Dorian shifts beside me which makes me break my eye contact with his mother.

"This is Ilana Kiri'gin. Ilana, these are my parents."

"It's lovely to meet you." I stretch my hand out to his mother first. She gently takes my hand and shakes it before letting go. I offer my hand to his father as well who shakes my hand with a little too much enthusiasm to the point where I nearly stumble forward a little. There's a small part of me that wants to use this opportunity to try and intimidate them. To try and subtly remind them that they killed a group of innocent people, but at the same time, the ritual helped clear most, but not all, of my hatred toward the Mother and the Father. Unfortunately, though, that's not why we're here so I have to remind myself to breathe. There will be time for revenge in the future, especially since I'm not planning on leaving Bordova anytime soon.

"Likewise. I must say though, I recognize your last name but for the life of me I can't think of where I've heard it before," his father says and I nod.

"I was part of the Children Rehomed initiative when I was nine. James and Phillip Kiri'gin are my parents."

The Father nods his head. "Yes, I think I remember now. You were on the way to the centre just as your, now, fathers were about to head home after this exact event. I remember because you looked so sad and then they saw you and heard that you needed a home. They decided then and there that they wanted to give you a home, which was quite unusual since it took a little while for most of the children to be rehomed."

I smile weakly, not sure I want to relive the worst and best week of my life with the man who had one of my closest friends killed.

"Oh, it's lovely to hear that you remember that, it was so long ago," I say, trying to keep back the nausea that has wormed its way through me at bay. Being nice to the Father is the last thing I wanted to do tonight.

The Father nods. "Well, we'll let you get on with the evening. It was lovely to meet you, Ilana."

"Likewise," I mutter as we turn and watch them leave.

"Want to go and steal a couple of paintings?" Dorian asks as he passes me a flute of something bubbly.

"Yes please," I say, downing the drink.

We put on the act of a giggling, in love couple. Dorian pulls me close to him and pretends to whisper something in my ear. I nod, looking at him, hopefully, as though he had hung the moon before we head toward one of the exits.

CHAPTER EIGHT

The guards don't bat an eyelash as Dorian drags me out of the ballroom. We run down the straight corridor, right past the second set of guards before he pulls me left, then right, left again and then through a grand archway. Once the orchestral music from the ballroom becomes faint, we stop running and take a leisurely walk to the gallery.

Dorian lets go of my hand and pushes open the heavy wooden doors. A small puff of dust flies from the doors as they move, indicating that this room hasn't been touched in a while. Dorian doesn't pull the doors all the way open though, just wide enough so that we can slip through.

Dorian takes hold of my hand again and pulls me over to the first painting.

"Start unscrewing the bolts," he orders. He hands me a screwdriver before wandering off.

I do as he says, unscrewing the bolts from the bottom of the frame. I struggle to reach the top bolts, and to be honest, I think Dorian would struggle to reach them without any kind of assistance. Luckily, he returns with a rickety looking ladder. He props it against the wall, slightly off centre to the middle of the painting before climbing it. I watch as he pulls out a second screwdriver and begins to unscrew the bolts at the top.

While he does that, I unhook the concealed pocket in my cape and take out the fake paintings. I carefully unroll them before flattening them out on the floor. I check them both for damage and wear. Thankfully, they appear to be in pristine condition.

"Come help me with the frame," Dorian calls and I quickly walk over to him.

I stand directly in the middle of the painting, my hands lightly grazing the edges of the large frame. He lifts the frame carefully before lowering it down to me. I struggle to support it on my own, but manage to place it safely on the floor.

Dorian makes light work of getting the painting off of the backboard before handing it down to me. I pass him the forgery and wait patiently as he tacks it back to the backboard. He motions for the frame. I stand the frame up with ease, but trying to lift it by myself is a bit of a struggle. After a few tries, and trialling several different hand placements, I manage to lift it and take it to Dorian. He pulls it up higher and we make quick work of reattaching it to the wall, but not before having one tiny, near job ruining hand slip. Thankfully though, we both had a good enough grip on the frame that it didn't fall too far.

I quickly screw in the bolts at the bottom while Dorian does the ones at the top. As soon as he's done, he climbs down the ladder before standing next to me.

"It's nice," he says.

"Nice? It looks like something Bolt leaves on the carpet."

Dorian rolls his eyes. "Roll up the original. I'll start on the second frame." He moves to the side and over to the next painting, then adds. "And roll it carefully."

"Yes mother," I mutter and roll my eyes. I,

carefully, roll the painting up before wrapping the twine Adeem provided us around the circumference.

Dorian seems to move with lightning speed because by the time I get to him he's already got the frame off and is untacking the painting. I quickly swipe the fake from the floor and hand it to him, taking the original from him at the same time. I move away and smooth the painting on the floor, checking again for wear and damage before rolling it up and securing it with the twine.

"Need any help?" I ask as I pick up the two rolled paintings.

"Nope. All done. Just need to put the ladder back," he says before wandering off with the ladder.

When he returns, I offer the two paintings to him. "Can you put them in the pocket, I don't want to damage them."

He nods and gestures for me to turn around. He lifts the cape at the back and tells me to take the corner from his hand. I hold it while he carefully slips the paintings into the pocket. Once that's done, he pops the hidden clasps together before telling me to let go of the cape. He fans the material out before coming round to my front and taking hold of my hand again.

"Good job," he says.

"Likewise," I respond with a slight smile pulling at my lips. As much as I hate Dorian, he's been extremely helpful with this job, and while I wouldn't admit it to his face, I don't think we'd have been able to do this without him.

We stand there for a moment, staring at each other in silence. In that silence, my mind flashes pictures of our interactions in the cells, and a question that has been niggling at the back of my mind reappears. He told me that he and Adeem were after similar things, but surely the paintings aren't what he's after? He's had access to them his entire life, so what is it that he's after?

"We better get moving," he says, breaking the silence and my thoughts.

I don't get the chance to say anything as he drags me toward the doors.

CHAPTER NINE

We exit the Gallery, carefully pulling the doors closed behind us.

"Dorian, wait a second," I say as I pull him behind a pillar.

"What?"

"In the cells, you said that you and Adeem were after similar things. Did you want a set of paintings as well?"

Dorian shakes his head. "I don't want the paintings, or any paintings for that matter. I want something that was taken by the Altaineian's during their retaliation to the siege."

"What did they take?"

He doesn't say anything.

"Tell me," I softly coax.

He runs a hand down his face. "They took my mother's jewellery box, along with other items, and I've received word that it's being kept in the palace."

I frown. "Is your mother bothered? She seemed more than content with the numerous bracelets she had on when we saw her."

He shakes his head. "Alessianna is my step mother. My biological mother died when giving birth to Grace. I was six at the time, but I remember the box so vividly. I've been working on getting it back for the last six months, the 20th anniversary of her death is coming up and I'd like to have it back."

I nod. "That's why you wanted me to tell you when Adeem cashed in my second job. You want to ask him to aid you in getting into the palace. You know you'll owe him, right?"

He nods. "As long as I get back the jewellery box, I don't care what Adeem asks of me."

"Dorian–" I'm cut off by the sound of heavy-duty boots on the marble floor.

"Guards," Dorian mutters and quickly grabs my waist and pulls me into view of the guards. "Laugh," he whispers into my ear.

I let out a little laugh before he tries to shush me with a smirk on his face, letting me know that he doesn't want me to stop.

"You said it, not me," I say, beginning the act as I hear the guards getting closer.

"Oh yeah? Are you challenging me, my *oveyli*?" he says and I roll my eyes, not impressed with him calling me *love*.

I smirk. "Oh, I'm challenging you, big time."

Dorian smirks, and suddenly his hand is wrapping around my throat just as the guards round the corner. He pulls me to him, and before I can even comprehend what is happening, his lips connect with mine. His free hand trails from the side of my face, down my neck and over my shoulder before settling on my lower back. He pulls me impossibly closer to him, and uses the hand on my lower back to keep me pinned to him. My whole body feels like it's on autopilot as he kisses me. The kiss is so overwhelming that nearly all of the oxygen leaves my lungs as I give into it. But I don't just give in to the kiss, I end up giving into Dorian himself when one of his hands works its way into my hair, tugging my head backwards to the point a small squeak escapes me. The brief thought that we are giving the guards quite a show runs through my mind as my hands grip at the lapels of Dorian's jacket.

"Guests shouldn't be down here," the first guard interrupts. Dorian pulls away and my brain short circuits. My whole body feels like it's on fire, and for some reason I feel like I need to be close to Dorian. And just as the thought crosses my mind, Dorian pulls me to him, one of his arms wrapping tightly around my waist.

"Surely the second son of the Father is allowed to roam around his home with his girlfriend, is he not?"

The guards exchanged scared facial expressions before bowing to Dorian.

"Our deepest apologies, Your Highness. We'll leave you to it," the second guard says. They make a quick exit.

We wait until we think they're out of ear shot before we burst into fits of laughter.

"The looks on their faces were priceless," he says as his laughter dies down.

I nod in agreement, but I'm still trying to recover

from that kiss.

Dorian kissed me.

I know it was to keep our cover intact, but what's freaking me out the most is the fact that I kind of enjoyed it. And that's something I was hoping wouldn't happen. I don't want to feel anything but hatred for Dorian, but after hearing his reasoning for doing this, and for the way he's been nothing but tolerant toward my outbursts, I can't help but feel sympathy for him. Deep down I know that Dorian is a good man and that his intentions that day in the cells were meant to be coming from a good place, but his timing was off. So incredibly off that we didn't get the chance to see if we could save Jake and the others, but I shake my head and clear my mind. Clear heads keep a job successful, and right now we need to focus on getting the paintings out of the House without getting stopped.

"Ready to go?" he asks as he checks the corridor ahead of us.

"Bones, yes," I say as he grabs my hand and I let him pull along behind him again.

CHAPTER TEN

My body and mind are completely exhausted when I crawl out of bed the next day.

I walk down the stairs at eight - o - clock, dressed and prepped for my final meeting with Adeem. I quickly grab some breakfast from the kitchen before heading to the safe and pulling out both paintings. They're still carefully rolled up as I place them on Beck's desk. I shut the safe behind me before grabbing the paintings and my breakfast before heading into the main club area.

"Good morning," Beck greets, as I round the bar and take a seat.

"Hi."

"You're chatty this morning," he says sarcastically.

"I'm tired and hungry. Talk to me again in about half an hour," I tell him as I shove a large piece of mango into my mouth.

Beck eyes me suspiciously. "Something happened last night, didn't it?

I shake my head. "I don't want to talk about last night, let alone think about it."

"Something juicy, I bet. Come on, tell me."

"No," I shove another piece of fruit in my mouth.

"Oh, come on–" He's cut off by the opening of the doors to the club and Adeem announcing his arrival. I roll my eyes at the theatrics before spinning on my barstool.

"Good morning, Adeem," I say as he comes and stands a few steps away from me. I slip off the barstool and stand level with him.

"It is indeed a lovely morning, Miss Kiri. But I won't be staying long since I have a boat to catch."

I nod and pick up the paintings. "Both paintings. No damage, no issues on retrieval and replacement. They're all yours, which means I don't owe you anything anymore. No more jobs, no more favours," I tell him as I move the paintings just out of his reach.

"You have my word Miss Kiri, the services you asked for have been paid back in full."

I nod, satisfied and hand him the paintings. At the same time, the door to the club opens and Dorian slips inside.

"Thank you, Miss Kiri. The palace will be extremely happy to have these back." He holds his hand out for me to shake, which I do.

"One last thing before I go," he says as he pulls an envelope out of his pocket and hands it to me. "If you feel up for another job, there's all the information."

"Whose it from?" Beck asks.

"It's from the Altaineian palace. I attempted this job, but I failed and was asked if I knew anyone who could help. You'd be doing a great service if you accept."

I nod. "We'll think about it."

"Goodbye, Miss Kiri," he says with a nod.

I watch as he heads toward the doors and I see Dorian catch his attention. The two of them leave the club and as soon as the door shuts, I slump back onto the barstool. I toss the envelope next to my plate and run my hands down my face.

"What's that?" Etta asks as she comes and sits next to me.

"What's what?"

"The envelope."

"It's a job, if we want it. A job being given out by the Altaineian palace."

"Good pay?" Ty asks as he slinks up next to Beck.

"I've no idea," I say.

"Well, let's open it and find out." Beck grabs the envelope and tears at the seal.

Want to read about the distraction Grace created?

Turn the page to find out what she did…

A. Carys

The Distraction

Causing a scene at the events my father holds is my favourite thing to do. I don't do it often, but when I do, they're spectacular.

"You think this will work?" Etta asks as we walk around the edges of the crowd.

I nod. "Ty naturally draws attention to himself, and causing a scene in public is right up his street."

"Beck told you, didn't he?" she questions, referencing the recent dust up at Harvey's Docks and Sailboat shop.

"He did. We got what we needed and everyone got out unseen, well, Ty did come out with a sprained wrist but that's beside the point. Everyone made it out alive so I believe he's the perfect person to do this with."

"Guess you don't hate him as much as you say you do," she teases, gently nudging me with her arm.

I roll my eyes. "Oh no, I still hate him. He knows how to rile me and I hate it."

"He does it on purpose, you know?"

"Well tell him to knock it off."

Etta laughs, throwing her head back. Once she stops laughing, we weave through the guests until we're close to the middle of the ballroom. I subtly look for Ty and it turns out that he's quite easy to spot. He's pulled his suit jacket off his shoulder and his tie has been loosened and moved to the side, making it look skewwhiff. His hair has been roughly tousled so that it's fluffy and pointing in various directions.

"Grace, Gracie my love?" he calls when he notices us. He stumbles toward us and calls out to me.

"Gracie please don't ignore me, please, please, please don't ignore me," he begs as Etta and I turn our backs. People start to glance at the three of us and I smile knowing that the distraction is working.

As Ty calls out to me again, I spot Dorian and Ilana looking ready to go. Dorian nods at me and I turn to face Ty.

"What Ty?" I ask.

"Don't leave me for her, my love. I love you," he slurs as he pretends to be drunk. "I love you, don't leave–"

"No. You cheated on me with my best friend the same night I told you I loved you," I yell which makes the guests turn and stare.

"Grace please. I'm sorry, it didn't mean anything I swear to you."

"Tyton, you and I are over," I say with a sniffle, pretending to get upset. "Please, just leave me alone."

He starts begging again as he reaches for me. His hand grazes my arm but I don't let him get any closer as my hand files out, a sharp smack fills the room. The guests gasp, their hands coming up to their chests and mouths, acting like they've been scandalised.

Guards from around the room flock to us and Ty is pulled up from his crumpled position on the floor. Everyone watches as he's dragged away and I note the hand print shape forming on his cheek. I look him in the eyes as the guards reach the doors to the ballroom and he winks at me, making me roll my eyes.

He enjoyed that. That idiot enjoyed being slapped.

"Come on, let's go mingle," Etta says as she pulls at my arm.

Language Glossary

Bordovan

En orr soulle tasp asfley ofro ell oland se ell givan op ell oland se ell decess. – May your soul pass safely from the land of the living to the land of the dead.

En ær ista passuno, hra yna vilgilan enkat ni orr amne astifi ell estlensess ni orr soulle. – May you rest peacefully, and any vengeance taken in your name satisfy the restlessness in your soul.

Ih lepsay - Oh please

Enfreynar – Hellhound

Oveyli – Love

A. Carys

ABOUT THE AUTHOR

A. Carys is a self-published author from Portsmouth, United Kingdom. Other than spending 90% of her day writing, she also loves to crochet, read, and take photos of her family's cats.

Printed in Great Britain
by Amazon